THE FAMILY CAR SONGBOOK

Hundreds of Miles of Fun!

RUNNING PRESS
PHILADELPHIA · LONDON

© 1983, 1991, 1998 by Running Press

All rights reserved under the Pan-American and International Copyright Conventions

Printed in China

This book may not be reproduced in whole or in part, in any form or by any means,
electronic or mechanical, including photocopying, recording, or by any information storage and
retrieval system now known or hereafter invented, without written permission from the publisher.

9   8   7   6   5   4   3

Digit on the right indicates the number of this printing

Library of Congress Cataloging-in-Publication Number 97-66833

ISBN 0-7624-0271-7

Cover Design by Maria Taffera Lewis
Designed by Frances J. Soo Ping Chow
Illustrated by Michael Gelen
Edited by Greg Jones

This book may be ordered by mail from the publisher.
Please include $2.50 for postage and handling.
But try your bookstore first!

Running Press Book Publishers
125 South Twenty-second Street
Philadelphia, Pennsylvania 19103-4399

Playlist

4 The Old Gray Mare
Traditional

6 Over the River and through the Woods
Traditional Thanksgiving song

8 America the Beautiful
Lyrics by Samuel A. Ward

10 The Marines' Hymn
Lyrics by I.Z. Phillips

12 I've Been Working on the Railroad
Traditional railroad song

15 Greensleeves
Traditional English folksong

18 My Darling Clementine
Lyrics by Percy Montrose

21 When Johnny Comes Marching Home
Lyrics by Louis Lambert

23 Yankee Doodle
Traditional

26 I Wish I Were in Dixie (Dixie Land)
Lyrics by Dan Decatur Emmett

29 America! (My Country, 'Tis of Thee)
Lyrics by Henry Carey

32 Shenandoah
Traditional bargeman's song

34 Git Along, Little Dogies
Traditional cowboy song

36 The Yellow Rose of Texas
Lyrics by "J.K."

38 Goober Peas
Lyrics by A. Pindar

40 The Streets of Laredo
Traditional cowboy song

43 Funiculi, Funicula
Lyrics by Edward Oxenford

45 Hush, Little Baby
Traditional Southern lullaby

47 Home on the Range
Traditional cowboy song

50 Little Brown Jug
Lyrics by "Eastburn"

52 Michael, Row the Boat Ashore
West Indian spiritual

54 She'll Be Comin' 'round the Mountain
Traditional railroad song

57 Swanee River (Old Folks at Home)
Lyrics by Stephen Collins Foster

59 Battle Hymn of the Republic
Lyrics by Julia Ward Howe

62 The Wabash Cannonball
Traditional hobo song

64 Kookaburra
Traditional Australian round

66 Jeanie with the Light Brown Hair
Lyrics by Stephen Collins Foster

68 Camptown Races (Going to Run All Night)
Lyrics by Stephen Collins Foster

70 Blow the Man Down
Traditional sea chanty

72 'Round Her Neck She Wears a Yeller Ribbon
Traditional

74 Oh, Susanna!
Lyrics by Stephen Collins Foster

76 Meet Me in St. Louis, Louis
Lyrics by Andrew B. Sterling

79 Home, Sweet Home
Lyrics by John Howard Payne

THE OLD GRAY MARE

Oh, the old gray mare, she ain't what she used to be, ain't what she used to be, ain't what she used to be. The old gray mare, she ain't what she used to be, many long years a - go____.

Chorus: Ma - ny long years a - go____, ma - ny long years a - go____, the old gray mare, she ain't what she used to be, ma - ny long years a - go____.

Oh, the old gray mare, she
Kicked on the wiffletree,
Kicked on the wiffletree,
Kicked on the wiffletree,

The old gray mare, she
Kicked on the wiffletree
Many long years ago.
Chorus

SHADY ACRES

5

Over the River and through the Woods

O - ver the ri - ver and through the woods to grand - mo - ther's house we go___. The

horse knows the way to car - ry the sleigh thru the white and drift - ed snow, oh!

O - ver the ri - ver and through the woods, oh how the wind doth blow___! It

stings the toes and bites the nose as o - ver the ground we go.

2 Over the river and through the woods
   To have a real day of play.
Oh, hear the bells ring, they ting-a-ling-ling,
   Because it's Thanksgiving Day.
Over the river and through the woods
   Trot fast, my dappled gray.
Spring over the ground just like a hound,
   For this is Thanksgiving Day.

3 Over the river and through the woods
   And straight through the barnyard gate.
We seem to be going ever so slow.
   It's so very hard to wait!
Over the river and through the woods
   Now grandmother's cap I spy.
Hooray for the fun! Are the puddings done?
   Hooray for the pumpkin pie!

AMERICA THE BEAUTIFUL

Oh beau - ti - ful for spa - cious skies, for am - ber waves of grain, for pur - ple moun - tain

ma - jes - ties a - bove the fruit - ed plain. A - mer - i - ca! A - mer - i - ca! God

shed his grace on thee and crown thy good with bro - ther - hood from sea to shin - ing sea.

3 Oh beautiful for pilgrim feet
Whose stern impassion'd stress,
A thoroughfare for freedom beat
Across the wilderness.
America! America!
    God mend thine every flaw.
Confirm thy soul in self-control,
Thy liberty in law.

3 Oh beautiful for heroes proved
In liberating strife,
Who more than self their country loved
And mercy more than life.
America! America!
    May God thy gold refine
Till all success be nobleness
And every gain divine.

3 Oh beautiful for patriot dream
That sees beyond the years,
Thine alabaster cities gleam
Undimmed by human tears.
America! America!
    God shed His grace on thee
And crown thy good
With brotherhood
From sea to shining sea.

The Marines' Hymn

From the Halls of Mon - te - zu - ma to the shores of Tri - po - li,

We will fight our count - ry's ba - ttles in the air, on land, and sea.

First to fight for right and free - dom and to keep our ho - nor clean.

We are proud to claim the ti - tle of the U - ni - ted States Ma - rine.

2) Our flag's unfurled to every breeze
From dawn to setting sun.
We have fought in every clime and place
Where we could take a gun.
In the snow of far-off northern lands
And in sunny tropic scenes,
You will find us always on the job—
The United States Marines.

3) Here's health to you and to our Corps
Which we are proud to serve.
In many a strife we've fought for life
And never lost our nerve.
If the Army and the Navy
Ever look at Heaven's scenes
They will find the streets are guarded
By United States Marines.

I've Been Working on the Railroad

I've been work-ing on the rail-road all the live-long day. I've been work-ing on the rail-road just to pass the time a-way. Don't you hear the whis-tle blow-ing? Rise up so ear-ly in the morn! Don't you hear the fore-man shou-ting? Di-nah, blow your horn!

(2) I've been working on the trestle,
Driving spikes that grip.
I've been working on the trestle
To be sure the ties won't slip.
Can't you hear the engine coming?
Run to the stanchion of the bridge!
Can't you see the big black smokestack
Coming down the ridge?

Chorus

(3) I've been living in the boxcars.
I'm a hobo now.
I've been living in the boxcars,
Which the yard bulls won't allow.
Brother, can you spare a quarter?
Buy me something good to eat?
Brother, can you spare a nickel,
Till I'm on my feet?

Chorus

(4) I'll be owner of this railroad
One of these here days.
I'll be owner of this railroad,
And I swear, your pay I'll raise.
I'll invite you to my mansion,
Feed you on goose and terrapin.
I'll invite you to the racetrack
When my ship comes in.

Chorus

GREENSLEEVES

A - las, my lo - ve! You do me wro - ng to cast me o - ff dis - court - eous - ly. For

I have loved you so ve - ry long ____, de - li - ght - ing in ____ your com - pa - ny.

Green - sle - eves was all my joy ____. Gre - en - sle - eves was my de - light.

Green - sleeves was my heart of gold ____, yea, who but my la - dy Green - sleeves?

2) I have been ready at your hand,
To grant whatever that you might crave.
I have wagered both life and land,
Your love and good-will for to have.
If you intend thus to disdain,
It doth the more enrapture me.
And even so, I still remain
Your lover in captivity.

3) My men were clothed all in green,
And they did ever attend on thee.
All this was gallant to be seen,
And yet, thou wouldst not love me.
Thou couldst desire no earthly thing,
But soon thou hadst it readily.
Thy music still I play and sing,
And yet thou wilt not love me.

4) Well, I shall petition God on high,
That thou my constancy mayest see,
And that yet once before I die,
That thou wilt vouchsafe to love me.
Ah, Greensleeves, farewell, adieu,
And God, I trust, shall prosper thee.
For I am still thy lover true.
Come back once more and love me.

5) Ye watchful guardians of the fair,
Who skim on wings of ambient air,
Of my dear Delia take a care,
And represent her lover
With all the gaiety of youth,
With honor, justice, love, and truth,
Till I return, her passions soothe.
For me in whispers move her.

6 Let all the world turn upside-down
And fools run an eternal round
In quest of what can ne'er be found,
To please their own ambitions.
Let little minds great charms espy
In shadows which at distance lie,
Whose hoped-for pleasure, when come nigh,
Proves nothing in fruition.

7 But cast into a mold divine,
Fair Delia does with luster shine.
Her virtuous soul's an ample mine
That yields a constant treasure.
Let poets in sublimest verse
Employ their skills, her frame rehearse,
Let sons of music pass whole days
With well-tuned flutes to please her.

My Darling Clementine

In a cavern, in a canyon, ex-ca-va-ting for a mine; dwelt a min-er, for-ty-

nin-er, and his daugh-ter, Clem-en-tine. Oh, my dar-ling, oh, my dar-ling, oh, my

Chorus:

dar-ling Clem-en-tine! You are lost and gone for-ev-er, dread-ful sor-ry, Clem-en-tine!

2 Light she was, and like a fairy,

And her shoes were number nine.

Herring boxes without topses,

Sandals were for Clementine.

Chorus

3 Drove she ducklings to the water

Every morning just at nine.

Struck her toes against a splinter,

Fell into the foaming brine.

Chorus

4 Ruby lips above the water

Blowing bubbles soft and fine.

Woe is me, I was no swimmer,

So I lost my Clementine.

Chorus

5 Then the miner, Forty-Niner,

He grew sad, began to pine,

Thought he oughter "jine" his daughter.

Now he's gone—like Clementine.

Chorus

6 In a churchyard, near the canyon,

Where the myrtle shoots entwine,
There grow rosies, 'n' other posies
Fertilized by Clementine.

Chorus

7 In my dreams she still doth haunt me,

Robed in garments soaked in brine.
Though in life I used to hug her,

Now she's dead, I'll draw the line.

Chorus

When Johnny Comes Marching Home

2. The old churchbell will peal with joy.
Hurrah! Hurrah!
To welcome home our darling boy.
Hurrah! Hurrah!
The village lads and lassies say
With roses they will strew the way.

Chorus

3. Get ready for the Jubilee.
Hurrah! Hurrah!
We'll give the hero
   Three times three.
Hurrah! Hurrah!
The laurel wreath is ready now
To place upon his loyal brow.

Chorus

4. Let love and friendship on that day.
Hurrah! Hurrah!
Their choiest treasures then display.
Hurrah! Hurrah!
And let each one perform some part
To fill with joy his warrior's heart.

Chorus

Yankee Doodle

Fa- ther and I went down to camp a - long with Cap - tain Good - win, and there we saw the

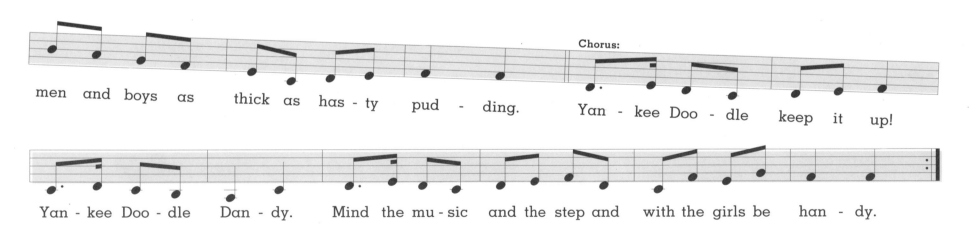

men and boys as thick as has - ty pud - ding.

Chorus:

Yan - kee Doo - dle keep it up!

Yan - kee Doo - dle Dan - dy. Mind the mu - sic and the step and with the girls be han - dy.

2 And there we saw a thousand men,
As rich as Squire David.
And what they wasted every day,
I wish it could be saved.

Chorus

3 And there was Captain Washington
Upon a strapping Stallion
A-giving orders to his men—
I guess there was a million.

Chorus

4 And then the feathers on his hat,
They looked so very fine, ah!
I wanted one of them to get,
To give to my Jemimah.

Chorus

5 And there I saw a swamping gun,
Large as a log of maple,
Upon a mighty little cart,
A load for father's cattle.

Chorus

6 And every time they fired it off,
It took a horn of powder.
It made a noise like father's gun,
Except a whole lot louder.

Chorus

7 And there I saw a little drum,
Its head's all made of leather.
They knocked upon't with little sticks
To call the troops together.

Chorus

8 And Captain Davis had a gun,
He clapped his hand upon it,
And stuck a crooked stabbing iron
Upon the little end on't.

Chorus

9 And Uncle Sam came there to charge
Some pancakes and some onions,
And 'lasses cakes to carry home
To give his wife and young ones.

Chorus

10 And there they'd fife away for fun
And play on cornstalk fiddles,
And some wore ribbons red as blood
Bound tight around their middles.

Chorus

11 The troopers, too, would gallop up
And shoot right in our faces.
It scared me almost half to death
To see them run such races.

Chorus

12 It scared me so that I ran off,
Nor stopped, as I remember,
Nor turned about till I gone home,
Locked up in mother's chambers.

Chorus

I Wish I Were in Dixie
(Dixie Land)

I wish I were in the land of cot-ton. Old times there are not for-got-ten. Look a-

way! Look a-way! Look a-way! Dix-ie Land. In Dix-ie Land where I was born in,

ear-ly on one fros-ty morn-in', look a-way! Look a-way! Look a-way! Dix-ie Land.

Chorus:

Then I wish I was in Dix-ie. Hoo-ray! Hoo-ray! In Dix-ie Land I'll take my stand, to

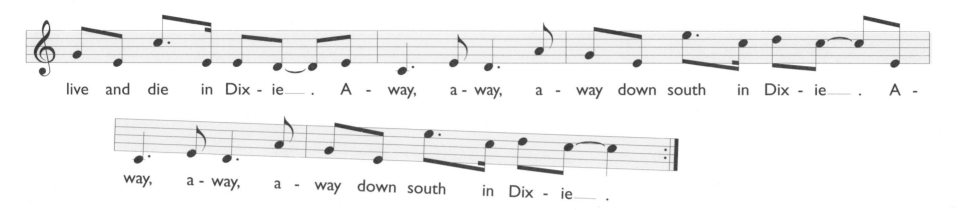

live and die in Dix - ie—. A - way, a - way, a - way down south in Dix - ie—. A -

way, a - way, a - way down south in Dix - ie—.

2 Old Missus married Will the Weaver.

William was a gay deceiver.

Look away! Look away!

Look away! Dixie Land.

But when he put his arm around her,

He smiled as fierce as

A forty-pounder.

Look away! Look away!

Look away! Dixie Land.

Chorus

3 His face was sharp as

A butcher's cleaver,

But that did not seem to grieve her.

Look away! Look away!

Look away! Dixie Land.

Old Missus acted the foolish part

And died for a man

That broke her heart.

Look away! Look away!

Look away! Dixie Land.

Chorus

4 Now here's a toast to

The next old Missus,

And all the girls that want to kiss us.

Look away! Look away!

Look away! Dixie Land.

But if you want to drive 'way sorrow,

Come and hear this song tomorrow.

Look away! Look away!

Look away! Dixie Land.

Chorus

5) There's buckwheat cakes and Injun batter,

Makes you fat or a little fatter.

Look away! Look away!

Look away! Dixie Land.

Then hoe it down and scratch your gravel.

To Dixie Land I'm bound to travel.

Look away! Look away!

Look away! Dixie Land.

Chorus

6) Gonna cook a meal of grits and taters,

Feed what's left to the alligators.

Look away! Look away!

Look away! Dixie Land.

And when I die, see that they lay me

'Neath an oak that's cool and shady.

Look away! Look away!

Look away! Dixie Land.

Chorus

America!

(My Country, 'Tis of Thee)

My coun - try 'tis of thee, sweet land of lib - er - ty, of thee I sing.

Land where my fa - thers died, land of the pil - grims' pride,

from ev - e - ry moun - tain - side let free - dom ring.

(2) My native country! Thee,
Land of the noble free,
Thy name I love.
I love thy rocks and rills,
Thy woods and templed hills.
My heart with rapture thrills,
Like that above.

(3) Let music swell the breeze
And sing from all the trees
Sweet freedom's song.
Let mortal tongues awake,
Let all that breathe partake,
Let rocks their silence break,
The sound prolong.

(4) Our father's God! To Thee,
Author of liberty,
To Thee we sing.
Long may our land be bright
With freedom's holy light.
Protect us by Thy might,
Great God our king.

(5) God bless our native land.
Firm may She ever stand,
Through storm and night.
When the wild tempests rave,
Ruler of wind and wave,
Do Thou our country save,
By Thy great might.

6. For Her our prayer shall rise
To God above the skies.
On Him we wait.
Thou, who are ever nigh,
Guarding with watchful eye,
To Thee aloud we cry,
"God save the state!"

7. Lord of all truth and right,
In Whom alone is might,
On Thee we call.
Give us prosperity,
Give us true liberty.
May all th' oppressed go free.
God save us all!

SHENANDOAH

Oh, Shen-an-doah, I love your daugh-ter___. A - way___, you roll-ing riv-er___. I'll

Chorus:

take her cross___ yon-der wa-ter___. A - way___, we're bound a-way. 'Cross the wide___ Mis-sou - ri.

2 Oh, Shenandoah,
  She took my fancy.
  Away, you rolling river.
Oh, Shenandoah,
  I love your Nancy.

Chorus

3 Oh Shenandoah,
  I long to see you.
  Away, you rolling river.
Oh, Shenandoah,
  I'm drawing near you.

Chorus

4 Oh, Shenandoah,
    I'm bound to leave you.
Away, you rolling river.
Oh, Shenandoah,
    I'll ne'er deceive you.

Chorus

5 Oh, Shenandoah,
    I'll ne'er forget you.
Away, you rolling river.
Oh, Shenandoah,
    I'll ever love you.

Chorus

Git Along, Little Dogies

As I was a-walk-ing one morn-ing for plea-sure, I spied a cow-punch-er come rid-ing a-long. His

hat was pushed back, and his spurs were a-jang-ling, and as he ap-proached, he was

Chorus:

sing-ing this song: Yip-pee-yah, hi yo! Git a-long lit-tle do-gies. It's your mis-for-tune and

none of my own. Yip-pee-yay, hi yo! Git a-long lit-tle do-gies, for you know Wy-o-ming-'ll be your new home.

2. It's early in spring when
   We round up the dogies,
We rope 'em and brand 'em
   And bob off their tails.
We water our ponies, load up
   The chuck-wagon,
And then drive the dogies
   Out onto the trail.

Chorus

3. Some boys, they go out
   On the trail just for pleasure,
But that's where they get it
   Most terribly wrong—
You'd never imagine
   The trouble they give us!
It takes all we've got
   To keep moving along.

Chorus

4. It's yelling and whooping
   And driving the dogies,
And oh, how we wish
   They would kindly move on.
It's whooping and punching
   And "Git on, little dogies,
For you know Wyoming must be
   Your new home."

Chorus

The Yellow Rose of Texas

There's a Yel-low Rose in Tex-as that I am go'ng to see. No oth-er fel-low knows her—, no,

not a one but me. She— cried so when I left her—, it like to broke my heart, and if I ev-er find her—, we

Chorus:

nev-er more will part. She's the sweet-est rose in Tex-as— that this man e-ver knew. Her

eyes are bright as dia-monds—. They spar-kle like the dew. You may talk a-bout your dear-est May and

sing of Ro-sa Lee, but the Yel-low Rose of Tex-as beats the belles of Ten-nes-see.

36

2 Where the Rio Grande is flowing
And starry skies are bright,
She walks along the river
In the quiet summer night.
She asks if I remember
When we parted long ago,
I promised to come back again,
And not to leave her so.

Chorus

3 Oh, now I'm going to find her
For my heart is full of woe.
We'll sing the songs together
We sung so long ago.
We'll play the banjo gaily,
We'll sing the songs of yore,
And the Yellow Rose of Texas
Will be mine forevermore.

Chorus

GOOBER PEAS

Sit - ting by the road - side on a sum - mer's day, chat - ting with my mess - mates,

pass - ing time a - way. Ly - ing in the shad - ows, un - der - neath the trees,

good - ness, how de - li - cious, eat - ing goo - ber peas! Peas, peas, peas, peas!

Eat - ing goo - ber peas! Good - ness, how de - li - cious, eat - ing goo - ber peas! (Repeats)

Chorus:

2) When a horseman rides by,
The soldiers have a rule,
To cry out at their loudest,
"Mister, here's your mule!"
But another pleasure
    Enchantinger than these
Is wearing out your grinders
Eating goober peas!

Chorus

3) Just before the battle
The General hears a row.
He says, "The Yanks are coming,
I hear their rifles now!"
He turns around in wonder,
    And what d'you think he sees?
The Georgia Militia
Eating goober peas!

Chorus

4) I think this song has lasted
Almost long enough.
The subject's interesting,
But rhyming's mighty rough.
I wish this war was over when,
    Free from rags and fleas,
We'll kiss our wives and sweethearts
And gobble goober peas.

Chorus

The Streets of Laredo

As I____ walked out in the streets of La - re - do, as I walked out in La - re - do one day, I spied a poor cow - boy wrapped up in white lin - en, wrapped up in white lin - en and cold as the clay.

(2) "I see by your outfit that you are a cowboy."
These words he did say as I boldly stepped by.
        "Come sit down beside me and hear my sad story—
I was shot in the chest and I know I must die.

(3) "Let sixteen gamblers come serve as my mourners.
Let sixteen cowboys come sing me a song.
        Take me to the graveyard and lay the sod o'er me,
For I'm a poor cowboy and I know I've done wrong.

(4) "It was once in the saddle I used to go dashing.
It was once in the saddle I'd ride all the day.
        'Twas first to drinking and then to card playing,
        Got shot in the chest, and I'm dying today.

(5) "Get six jolly cowboys to carry my coffin.
Get six pretty maids to carry my pall.
        Put bunches of roses all over my coffin,
White roses to soften the clods as they fall.

6 "Oh, beat the drum slowly and play the fife lowly
And play a sad dirge as you tote me along.
Take me to the valley and lay the earth o'er me,
For I'm a young cowpoke and I know I've done wrong."

7 We beat the drum slowly and played the fife lowly,
And bitterly wept as we bore him along.
For we all loved our comrade, so brave and so handsome,
We all loved our cowboy although he'd done wrong.

FUNICULI, FUNICULA

Some think the world is made for fun and fro - lic. And so do I! And so do

I! Some think it well to be all mel - an - chol - ic, to pine and sigh, to pine and sigh. But

I, I love to spend my time in sing - ing. Some joy - ous song to set the air with mu - sic brave - ly

Chorus:

ring - ing is far from wrong, is far from wrong____! Lis - ten! Lis - ten! Ech - oes sound a - far! Lis - ten! Lis - ten! Ech - oes sound a -

far! Fu - nic - u - li, fu - nic - u - la. Fu - nic - u - li, fu - nic - u - la, ech - oes sound a - far! Fu - nic - u - li, fu - nic - u - la.

2 Some think it wrong to set the feet a-dancing!
But not so I, but not so I!
Some think that eyes should keep from coyly glancing
Upon the sly, upon the sly!
But oh, to me the mazy dance is charming,
Divinely sweet, divinely sweet!
For surely there is nought that is alarming
In nimble feet, in nimble feet!

Chorus

3 Ah, me! 'Tis strange that some should take to sighing,
And like it well, and like it well!
For me, I have not thought it worth the trying,
So cannot tell, so cannot tell!
With laugh and dance and song the day soon passes,
Full soon is gone, full soon is gone!
For mirth was made for joyous lads and lasses
To call their own, to call their own!

Chorus

Hush, Little Baby

Hush, lit-tle ba-by, don't say a word. Dad-dy's gon-na buy you a mock-ing-bird. And

if that mock-ing - bird don't sing, Dad-dy's gon-na buy you a dia-mond ring.

2 If that diamond ring turns to brass,
Daddy's gonna buy you a looking glass.
If that looking glass gets broke,
Daddy's gonna buy you a nanny goat.

3 If that goat don't give no milk,
Daddy's gonna buy you a robe of silk.
If that robe of silk gets worn,
Daddy's gonna buy you a big French horn.

4 If that big French horn won't play,
Daddy's gonna buy you a candy cane.
If that cane should lose its stripes,
Daddy's gonna buy you a set of pipes.

5 If that set of pipes ain't clean,
Daddy's gonna buy you a jumping bean.
If that jumping bean won't roll,
Daddy's gonna buy you a lump of coal.

6 If that lump of coal won't burn,
Daddy's gonna buy you a butter churn.
If that butter turns out sour,
Daddy's gonna buy you an orchid flower.

7 If that flower don't smell sweet,
Daddy's gonna buy you some salted meat.
If that salted meat won't fry,
Daddy's gonna buy you an apple pie.

8 When that apple pie's all done,
Daddy's gonna buy you another one.
When that pie's all eaten up,
Daddy's gonna buy you a greyhound pup.

9 If that dog won't run the course,
Daddy's gonna buy you a rocking horse.
If that rocking horse won't rock,
Daddy's gonna buy you a cuckoo clock.

HOME ON THE RANGE

Oh, give me a home where the buf - fa - lo roam, where the deer and the an - te - lope play,

where sel - dom is heard a dis - cour - ag - ing word, and the sky is not clou - ded all day.

Chorus:

Home, home on the range, where the deer and the an - te - lope play, where

sel - dom is heard a dis - cour - a - ging word, and the sky is not cloud - ed all day.

2 Oh, give me a gale on some soft Southern vale,

Where the stream of life joyfully flows,

On the banks of the river, where seldom if ever,

any poisonous herbiage grows.

Chorus

3 Oh, give me a land where the bright diamond sands
Lie awash in the glittering stream,
Where days glide along in leisure and song,

And afternoons pass as a dream.

Chorus

4 I love the bright flowers in this frontier of ours,
And I thrill to the eagle's shrill scream.

Blood red are the rocks, brown the antelope flocks
That browse on the prairie so green.

Chorus

5 The breezes are pure, and the sky is azure,
And the zephyrs so balmy and slow,
That I would not exchange my home on the range
For a townhouse in San Francisco.

Chorus

6 How often at night, when the heavens are bright
With the light of the unclouded stars,
Have I stood here amazed, and asked as I gazed,
If their glory exceeds that of ours.

Chorus

BUFFALO
ROAMING
PLEASE WATCH
YOUR STEP.

Little Brown Jug

My wife and I lived all a - lone in a lit - tle log hut we

called our own. She loved gin and I loved rum. I tell you what, we'd lots of fun!

Chorus:

Ha, ha, ha, you and me, lit - tle brown jug don't I love thee.

Ha, ha, ha, you and me, lit - tle brown jug don't I love thee.

2. 'Tis you who makes my friends my foes,
   'Tis you who makes me wear old clothes.
   Here you are, so near my nose,
   So tip her up and down she goes.

   Chorus

3. When I go toiling to my farm,
   I take little brown jug under my arm.
   I place it under a shady tree.
   Little brown jug, 'tis you and me.

   Chorus

4. If all the folks in Adam's race
   Were gathered together in one place,
   Then I'd prepare to shed a tear
   Before I'd part from you, my dear.

   Chorus

5. If I'd a cow that gave such milk,
   I'd clothe her in the finest silk.
   I'd feed her on the choicest hay,
   And milk her forty times a day.

   Chorus

Michael, Row the Boat Ashore

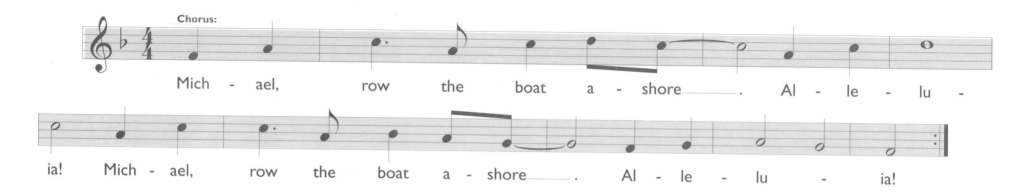

Chorus:

Mich - ael, row the boat a - shore____ . Al - le - lu -
ia! Mich - ael, row the boat a - shore____ . Al - le - lu - ia!

1. The River Jordan is chilly and cold,
   Alleluia!
   Chills the body, but not the soul,
   Alleluia!

   Chorus

2. River is deep, and the river is wide,
   Alleluia!
   Milk and honey on the other side,
   Alleluia!

   Chorus

(3) Brother, help me trim the sail,
Alleluia!
If we've faith, we cannot fail,
Alleluia!

Chorus

(4) River is quick, and the river is fast,
Alleluia!
But we shall reach that shore at last,
Alleluia!

Chorus

(5) Skies are black, and the wind's northwest,
Alleluia!
Grip that tiller and do your best,
Alleluia!

Chorus

(6) Sister, help him lock the oar,
Alleluia!
And he'll row the boat ashore,
Alleluia!

Chorus

She'll Be Comin' 'round the Mountain

She'll be com-in' 'round the moun-tain when she comes. She'll be com-in' 'round the moun-tain when she comes. She'll be com - in' 'round the moun - tain, she'll be com - in' 'round the moun - tain, she'll be com - in' 'round the moun - tain when she comes.

2 She'll be driving six white horses
When she comes.
She'll be driving six white horses
When she comes.
She'll be driving six white horses,
She'll be driving six white horses,
She'll be driving six white horses
When she comes.

3 She'll be shining bright as silver
When she comes.
She'll be shining bright as silver
When she comes.
She'll be shining bright as silver,
She'll be shining bright as silver,
She'll be shining bright as silver
When she comes.

4 She will neither rock nor totter
When she comes.
She will neither rock nor totter
When she comes.
She will neither rock nor totter,
She will neither rock nor totter,
She will neither rock nor totter
When she comes.

5 Oh, we'll all go out to meet her
When she comes.
Oh, we'll all go out to meet her
When she comes.
Oh, we'll all go out to meet her,
Oh, we'll all go out to meet her,
Oh, we'll all go out to meet her
When she comes.

6 We will kill the old red rooster
When she comes.
We will kill the old red rooster
When she comes.
We will kill the old red rooster,
We will kill the old red rooster,
We will kill the old red rooster
When she comes.

7 And we'll all have chicken and dumplings
When she comes.
And we'll all have chicken and dumplings
When she comes.
And we'll all have chicken and dumplings,
And we'll all have chicken and dumplings,
And we'll all have chicken and dumplings
When she comes.

8. There'll be joy and smiles and laughter
When she comes.
There'll be joy and smiles and laughter
When she comes.
There'll be joy and smiles and laughter,
There'll be joy and smiles and laughter,
There'll be joy and smiles and laughter
When she comes.

9. She will drive us all to Heaven
When she comes.
She will drive us all to Heaven
When she comes.
She will drive us all to Heaven,
She will drive us all to Heaven,
She will drive us all to Heaven
When she comes.

10. But it may be just a while yet
'Fore she comes.
Yes, it may be just a while yet
'Fore she comes.
Oh, it may be just a while yet,
Yes, it may be just a while yet,
And it may be just a while yet
'Fore she comes.

Swanee River

(Old Folks at Home)

Way down up-on the Swa-nee Riv-er, far, far a - way, that's where my heart is turn-ing ev-er,

there's where the old folks stay. All up and down the whole cre - a - tion, sad - ly I roam,

Chorus:

still long-ing for the old plan-ta-tion and for the old folks at home. All the world is sad and drea-ry,

ev - 'ry - where I roam. Oh, wit - ness how my heart grows wea-ry, far from the old folks at home.

2 All 'round the little farm I wandered,
When I was young.
Then, many happy days I squandered,
Many the songs I sung.
When I was playing with my brother,
Happy was I.
Oh, take me to my kind old mother,
There let me live and die.

Chorus

3 One little hut among the bushes,
One that I love,
Still sadly to my memory rushes
No matter where I rove.
When will I see the bees a-humming
All 'round the comb?
When will I hear the banjo strumming
Down in my dear old home?

Chorus

Battle Hymn of the Republic

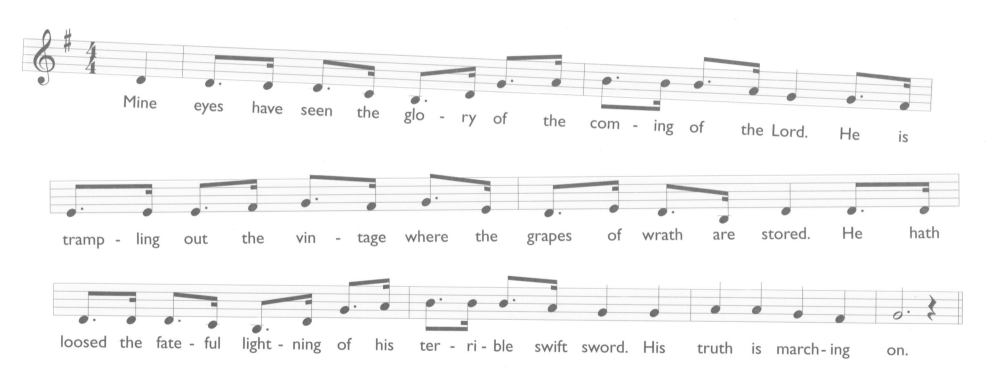

Chorus: Glo - ry! Glo - ry hal - le - lu - jah! Glo - ry! Glo - ry hal - le - lu - jah!

Glo - ry! Glo - ry hal - le - lu - jah! His truth is march - ing on.

2) I have seen Him in the watchfires
Of a hundred circling camps.
They have builded Him an altar
In the evening dews and damps.
I can read His righteous sentence
By the dim and flaring lamps.
His day is marching on.

Chorus

3) I have read a fiery gospel
Writ in burnished rows of steel:
"As ye deal with My condemnors,
So with ye My grace shall deal."
Let the hero born of woman
Crush the serpent with his heel,
Since God is marching on.

Chorus

4 He has sounded forth the trumpet
That shall never call retreat.
He is sifting out the hearts of men
Before His judgment seat.
Oh be swift, my soul, to answer Him!
Be jubilant, my feet!
Our God is marching on.

Chorus

5 In the beauty of the lilies
Christ was born across the sea,
With a glory in His bosom
That transfigures you and me.
As He died to make men holy
Let us die to make men free,
While God is marching on.

Chorus

THE WABASH CANNONBALL

From the great At - lan - tic O - cean to the wide Pa - cif - ic shore, from the green of bloom - ing moun - tains to the i - vy by the door, she's a migh - ty tall and hand-some and quite well - known by all. She's the mod-ern com - bin - na - tion on the Wa - bash Can - non - ball!

Chorus:

2 She came down from Birmingham
One cold December day.
As she rolled into the station,
You could hear the people say
"There's a girl from Tennessee.
She's long and she is tall.
She came down from Memphis—
Chorus

3 Now the eastern states are dandy,
So the western people say.
From New York to St. Louis,
And Chicago on the way,
From the hills of Minnesota
Where the rippling waters fall,
No chances can be taken—
Chorus

4 Will you listen to the whistle
And the rumble and the roar,
As she glides along the woodland,
Through the hills and by the shore.
Hear the throb of her great engine,
Hear the lonesome hobos squall,
"You're traveling through the jungle—
Chorus

Kookaburra

Koo - ka - bur - ra sits in the old gum tree___ .

Mer-ry, mer-ry king of the bush is he___ .

Laugh, Koo - ka - bur - ra, laugh, Koo - ka - bur - ra,

gay your life must be.

Kookaburra sits in an old gum tree,

Eating all the gumdrops he can see.

Stop, Kookaburra,

Stop, Kookaburra,

Leave a few for me.

Jeanie with the Light Brown Hair

I dream of Jean-ie with the light brown hair, borne like a va-por on the gold-en air. I see her trip-ping where the bright streams play, gay as the flow-ers a - long her way.

Chorus:

Ma-ny are the fond notes her mer-ry voice would pour, ech-oed by the birds in the grove o'er and o'er. Ah! I dream of Jean-ie with the light brown hair, a - float like va-por on the soft sum-mer air.

2 I long for Jeanie
With the day-dawn smile,
Radiant with gladness,
Warm with winning guile.
I hear her melodies
Attuned to love,
Warm as the sunlight
Lighting Heav'n above.

Chorus

3 I sigh for Jeanie
When the daylight fades,
Hour when the shadow
Haunts the dewy glades.
And when the stars
Adorn the midnight skies,
I view their light
As her own dear eyes.

Chorus

4 Sighing like the night wind,
And sobbing like the rain,
Waiting for my lost one
Who comes not again.
How I long for Jeanie
With my heart bowed low,
Never more to find her
Where the bright waters flow.

Chorus

Camptown Races
(Going to Run All Night)

The Camp-town la-dies sing this song: Doo-dah! Doo-dah! Camp-town race-track's five miles long.

Oh! Doo-dah day! I came down there with my hat caved in. Doo-dah! Doo-dah! I

went back home with a pock-et full of tin. Oh! Doo-dah day! Go-ing to run all night!

Go-ing to run all day! I'll bet my mo-ney on the bob-tail nag; some-bo-dy bet on the bay.

Chorus:

2. The long-tail filly and the big black horse—
    Doo-dah! Doo-dah!
They fly the track and they both cut across.
    Oh! Doo-dah day!
The blind horse wallowed in a big mud hole.
    Doo-dah! Doo-dah!
Can't touch bottom with a ten-foot pole.
    Oh! Doo-dah day!

Chorus

3. Old muley cow came onto the track.
    Doo-dah! Doo-dah!
The bobtail flung her over his back.
    Oh! Doo-dah day!
Then flew along like a railroad car.
    Doo-dah! Doo-dah!
Running a race with a shooting star.
    Oh! Doo-dah day!

Chorus

4. See them flying on a ten-mile heat—
    Doo-dah! Doo-dah!
'Round the racetrack, then repeat.
    Oh! Doo-dah day!
I won my money on the bobtail nag.
    Doo-dah! Doo-dah!
I keep my money in an old tow-bag.
    Oh! Doo-dah day!

Chorus

BLOW THE MAN DOWN

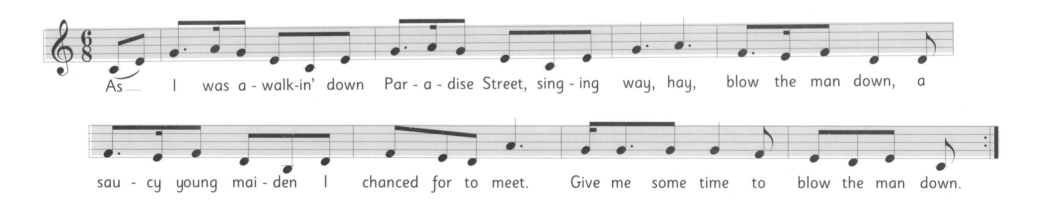

As— I was a-walk-in' down Par-a-dise Street, sing-ing way, hay, blow the man down, a sau-cy young mai-den I chanced for to meet. Give me some time to blow the man down.

2) I asked, "Where're you bound?" She said, "Nowhere today."
Singing way, hay, blow the man down.
"Now that's fine," I replied, "for I'm headed that way."
Give me some time to blow the man down.

3) We entered an ale-house, looked down on the sea.
Singing way, hay, blow the man down.
There stood a policeman who stared right at me.
Give me some time to blow the man down.

4. Said he, "You're a pirate that flies the black flag."
Singing way, hay, blow the man down.
"You've robbed some poor Dutchmen and left them in rags."
Give me some time to blow the man down.

5. "Oh, Officer, Officer, you do me wrong."
Singing way, hay, blow the man down.
"I'm a freshwater sailor just in from Hong Kong."
Give me some time to blow the man down.

6. But they jailed me six months in Old Lexington Town,
Singing way, hay, blow the man down,
For fighting and kicking and knocking him down.
Give me some time to blow the man down.

7. Come all you brave sailors who follow the sea,
Singing way, hay, blow the man down,
And join in a singing this chanty with me!
Give me some time to blow the man down!

'Round Her Neck She Wears a Yeller Ribbon

'Round her neck she wears a yel - ler rib - bon. She wears it in the spring - time and

in the month of May. And if you ask her, "Why the dec - o - ra-tion?" She'll say it's for her lov - er who is

fur, fur a - way! Fur a - way! Fur a - way! She wears it for her lov - er who is fur, fur a-way.

2. 'Round the park
   She walks a little baby.
She walks him in the winter
And the summer, so they say.
And if you ask her why on earth
   She walks him,
She walks him for her lover
Who is fur, fur away!
Fur away! Fur away!
She walks him for her lover
   Who is fur, fur away.

3. That boy,
   He is a cunning little feller.
His birthday was a year ago,
Late in the month of May.
And if you ask him,
   "Sonny, who's your daddy?"
He'll say, "My dad's a cowboy
Who is fur, fur away!
Fur away! Fur away!"
He'll say, "My dad's a cowboy
   Who is fur, fur away."

4. Behind the door
   Her father keeps a shotgun.
It's loaded with a double dose
Of buckshot, so they say.
And if you ask him,
   "Why the ammunition?"
He keeps it for that cowboy
Who is fur, fur away!
Fur away! Fur away!
He keeps it for that cowboy
   Who is fur, fur away.

Oh, Susanna!

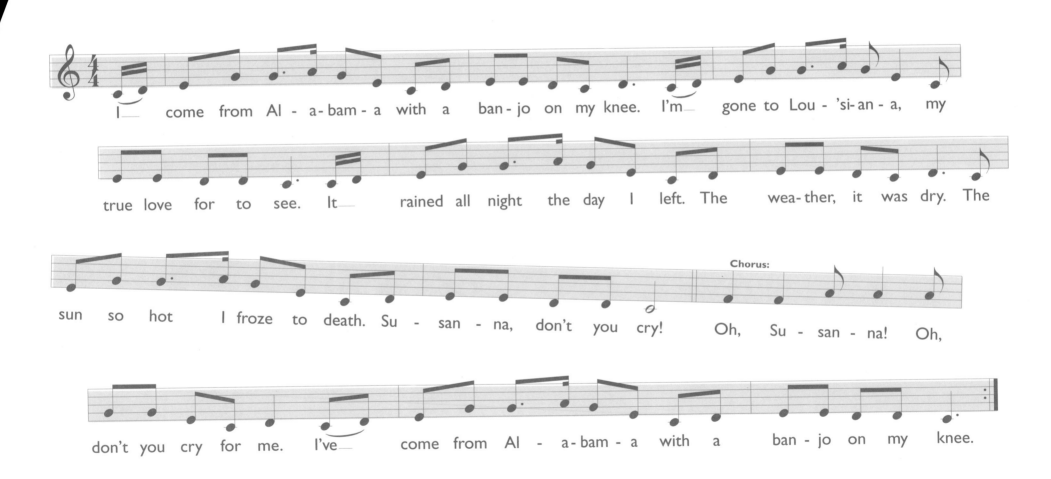

I come from Al - a-bam - a with a ban-jo on my knee. I'm gone to Lou - 'si-an - a, my

true love for to see. It rained all night the day I left. The wea-ther, it was dry. The

sun so hot I froze to death. Su - san - na, don't you cry! Oh, Su - san - na! Oh,

Chorus:

don't you cry for me. I've come from Al - a-bam - a with a ban - jo on my knee.

2) I jumped aboard the telegraph
And traveled down the wires.
The 'lectric fluid magnified
And lit five hundred fires.
The full moon burst; my horse ran off.
I really thought I'd die.
I shut my eyes to hold my breath.
Susanna, don't you cry!

Chorus

3) I had a dream the other night
When everything was still.
I thought I saw Susanna
A-coming down the hill.
A buckwheat cake was in her mouth;
A tear was in her eye.
I said, "I'm coming from the South,
Susanna, don't you cry!"

Chorus

4) I soon will be in New Orleans,
And then I'll look around,
And when I find Susanna
I'll fall upon the ground.
But if I do not find my love,
Then surely I shall die.
But when I'm dead and six feet down,
Susanna, don't you cry!

Chorus

Meet Me In St. Louis, Louis

When Lou - is came to the flat___, he hung up his coat and his hat___. He gazed all a - round, but no wi - fey he found, so he asked, "Where can Flos-sie be at___?" A note on the ta - ble he spied___. He read it just once, then he cried___. It

ran, "Lou - is dear, it's too slow for me here, so I think I will go for a ride___ .

Meet me in St. Lou - is, Lou - is, meet me at the fair___ .

Don't tell me that lights are shin - ing a - ny place but there___ . We will

dance the Hoot - chee Koot - chie___ , I will be your toot - sie woot - sie,

if you will meet me in St. Lou - is, Lou - is, meet me at the fair___ ."

77

The dresses that hung in the hall

Were gone—she had taken them all.

She took all his rings, and the rest of his things;

The picture he missed from the wall.

"What, moving?" the janitor said.

"Your rent is paid three months ahead!"

"What good is the flat?"

Asked poor Louis, "Read that!"

And the janitor smiled as he read:

Chorus

HOME, SWEET HOME

'Midst pleas-ures and pal-a-ces though we may roam, be it ev-er so hum-ble, there's

no place like home! A charm from the skies seems to hal-low us there, which,

seek through the world, I ne'er met with else-where. Home! Home!

Chorus:

Sweet, sweet home! There's no place like home! There's no place like home!

2 I gaze on the moon
As I tread the drear wild,
And feel that my mother
Now thinks of her child;
As she looks on that moon
From our own cottage door
Through the woodbine whose fragrance
Will cheer me no more.

Chorus

3 How sweet 'tis to sit
'Neath a fond father's smile,
The caress of a mother
To soothe and beguile.
Let others delight
'Midst new pleasures to roam,
But give me, oh, give me
The pleasures of home.

Chorus

4 To thence I'll return,
Overburdened with care.
My heart's dearest solace
Will smile on me there.
No more from that cottage
Again will I roam.
Be it ever so humble,
There's no place like home!

Chorus